Bedtime Fairy Stories: A Treasury

Little, Brown and Company

Hachette Book Group
1290 Avenue of the Americas, New York, NY 10019
Visit our website at lb-kids.com

LB kids is an imprint of Little, Brown and Company.
The LB kids name and logo are trademarks of
Hachette Book Group, Inc.

The publisher is not responsible for websites (or their content) that are not owned by the publisher.

First Edition: October 2014
A Lake in Pixie Hollow, *Picture Perfect*, and *Finders Keepers* originally published in 2006
by Disney Press, an imprint of Disney Book Group.
A Snowy Surprise, *Tink and the Messy Mystery*, and *The Great Fairy Camp Out*
originally published in 2008 by Disney Press, an imprint of Disney Book Group.
The Pixie Mix-Up originally published in 2007 by Disney Press, an imprint of Disney Book Group.
The Perfect Pumpkin Hunt originally published in 2012 by Random House Children's Books,
a division of Random House, Inc.
Beck's Bunny Secret originally published in 2010 by Random House Children's Books,
a division of Random House, Inc.

Library of Congress Control Number: 2014934948

ISBN 978-0-316-28339-7

10 9 8 7 6 5 4 3 2 1

IM

Printed in Malaysia

Disney Fairies

Bedtime Fairy Stories: A Treasury

LITTLE, BROWN & COMPANY

LB kids

Table of Contents

A Lake in Pixie Hollow

Early one morning in Pixie Hollow, Rani hurried down the stairs of the Pixie Dust Tree on her way to see Tinker Bell. She wasn't looking where she was going and suddenly...

Splash!

Rani looked down. She was standing in water.

"Oh my!" Rani exclaimed. "The dishes are floating away."

"The dishes aren't the only things floating away!" someone cried.

Rani peeked through the tunnel to find Dulcie bobbing across the water in a large pot.

"All of Pixie Hollow is flooded," Dulcie said.

Just then, they heard someone shouting in the distance. "Help!" cried Lily.

Rani hopped into the large pot with Dulcie and paddled outside. They found Lily trying to rescue a nest of chicks that had fallen into the water.

"The nest is too heavy!" Lily exclaimed. "Can you help me pull it in?"

As fast as they could, Rani and Dulcie grabbed on and helped pull the chicks to safety.

Once the chicks were safe and dry, Rani remembered
she was on her way to see Tinker Bell. "I have to go!" Rani
exclaimed. "Dulcie, can I please borrow your pot and spoon?"

"Of course," Dulcie answered. "My wings are nearly dry
now. Soon I'll be able to fly again."

Rani climbed back into the pot and started to drift away.

"There is a dent in one of the handles," Dulcie shouted.
"Would you ask Tink to—"

"Fix it? She would love to!" Rani said, and paddled off.

Rani arrived at Tink's house and knocked on the door.
When Tink opened it, she found Rani and a school of
minnows leaping outside her workshop!

Charmed by the minnows, Tinker Bell held out a
shiny silver spoon to attract more of the cute critters. As
she lowered the spoon into the water, Spring, a messenger-
talent fairy, arrived.

"Beck needs your help," Spring told Tink and Rani.
"Climb aboard. I will take you to her!"

On their way to help Beck, the fairies spotted Terence, who looked a little worried.

"The pixie dust is all wet," he said. "It could take days to dry out. Until then, no one will be able to fly!"

"Could the water fairies be of help?" Rani asked.

Nearby, some water fairies were dipping their hands in the lake and creating beautiful fountains. They were happy to see so much water.

"Of course!" cried Terence. "We can get around using the water fairies' leaf boats."

While Terence, Tink, and the water fairies delivered the leaf boats throughout Pixie Hollow, Rani hurried off to help Beck.

She found Beck in a Pixie Tree stairway trying to help three chipmunks stay dry.

"The chipmunks have nowhere to live," Beck shouted. "Their house is flooded. Can't you do something about this water? You're a water-talent fairy, Rani."

"I don't know where it is coming from," Rani admitted. "But we are all working together to get Pixie Hollow back to normal."

Two days later, Pixie Hollow was still flooded. But the fairies were starting to get used to the new lake.

The animal-talent fairies asked spiders to weave walkways and birds to carry tools.

The garden-talent fairies moved their plants and vegetables high above the lake to keep them safe. And all the fairies were becoming experts at leaf boating!

"Rani! Rani!" Beck called. "I just got done talking to my squirrel friends, and they told me what is causing the flood!"

"What is it?" Rani asked.

"Beavers have built a dam across the stream, and it's backed up all the way to Pixie Hollow," Beck explained. "I would go talk to them, but it's too far by leaf boat. And my turtle friend is too tired."

"Brother Dove can take us!" Rani said.

Rani whistled for Brother Dove. He arrived right away, and the two fairies climbed onto his back. Brother Dove took off, and the fairies were soaring fast above the water.

"Look!" Rani called out. "There is the dam."

Rani and Beck could now see the beaver dam and how the water had risen over the banks and flooded Pixie Hollow.

Brother Dove set Rani and Beck down on top of the dam.

"Hello," Beck said. There was a splash, and then three brown heads poked out of the water.

Beck talked to the beavers in their beaver language, explaining the flood in Pixie Hollow.

"We need your help," Beck said. "We need you to take down your dam and move it upstream so the water can flow through here."

"What do they say?" asked Rani.

"They say it is no problem!" responded Beck.

The next day, the water receded, and all was back to normal in Pixie Hollow.

Rani found Tink standing next to a leaf boat, looking upset.

"What's wrong?" Rani asked.

"It's just…" Tink started. "I was getting used to the lake in Pixie Hollow. And I miss the minnows at my doorstep."

"Dulcie just said the same thing," Rani said. "Maybe there is something I can do for all of you."

The following day, Rani arrived at Tink's workshop. "Come with me," she said. "And bring a shiny silver spoon."

Rani led Tink to a field that she had transformed into a fairy-sized lake! Some fairies paddled through the water on leaf boats while others waded at the edge.

"My minnows!" cried Tink.

"We decided to make our very own lake," Rani said. "So we would never forget the flood—the good parts at least!"

The End

Picture Perfect

Bess whistled as she flew through the garden. It was a beautiful morning, and she was in a cheery mood!

"Hello, Bess," Fira said. "Where are you off to?"

"I am headed to my new art studio," Bess replied. "I want to make a pretty painting to hang on my wall—something that will inspire me every time I see it!"

"That sounds like a wonderful plan!" Fira exclaimed.

Just as Bess flew away, Rani came walking through the garden.

"Where is Bess going?" she asked.

"Bess is off to her new art studio," Fira said. "She said she needs some inspiration."

"I know exactly what she needs!" Rani said excitedly. "See you later, Fira!"

With that, Rani hurried off toward a stream.

"It's perfect," Rani said to herself as she gathered a drop of water from the lake.

"What's perfect?" asked Tinker Bell.

Rani smiled. "This!" she exclaimed, holding up the drop of water. "Bess is in need of some inspiration, and what's more inspiring than beautiful blue water?"

"Inspiration, hmm?" Tink whispered to herself. Whenever Tink needed inspiration, she just looked at her shiny pots, pans, and Never silver. "That's it!" Tink said. "I know just what Bess needs."

In no time, Tink was on her way to Bess's workshop, carrying a large, shiny copper pot.

"Where are you taking that dazzling pot?" Lily asked. "Let me help you."

"I am taking it to Bess for inspiration," Tink explained.

"Inspiration?" Lily paused. "Wait! Come with me to my garden to get flowers for Bess. My violets are very inspiring."

Tink and Lily flew back to the violet patch and selected the most beautiful of the flowers.

As Tink and Lily flew over Pixie Hollow, Beck spotted the two fairies from a tree branch.

"Where are you headed with those beautiful violets and that copper pot?" Beck asked.

"We're taking it to Bess," Lily explained. "Sorry we can't stop, but she needs some inspiration right away!"

"Did you hear that?" Beck asked her squirrel friend.

The squirrel chattered and twitched his fluffy tail.

"Now, I'm not saying an acorn isn't inspiring," Beck responded, "but I have something else in mind."

Meanwhile, Bess had arrived at her art studio. *"This is going to be so exciting!"* she sang.

Bess had built her studio out of an old tangerine crate that washed up on the shore of Never Land. She decorated it with flowers and placed it in a quiet corner of the woods.

"Ah, with no interruptions or distractions, I can really start painting out here!" she sighed.

Bess sat down and stared at the white canvas in front of her. She held up her paintbrush and got ready to make the first stroke—but she couldn't decide what to paint.

"That's odd," Bess said to herself. "I usually have so many ideas for my paintings, but today my mind feels blank."

"Should I paint a flower?" she asked herself. "Or a tree? Maybe I can paint a sunset. Or I can paint a bluebird. How about I paint upside down?"

Bess thought of lots of things, but she wanted something very special for her wall. Something perfect.

"Why am I not feeling inspired?" Bess wondered.

Suddenly, there was a rustling in the bushes. Her fairy friends emerged, each carrying a gift.

"I brought you a drop of water to inspire you," said Rani.

"I brought you a speckled eggshell," said Beck. "You can use it to mix paint in."

"We brought you violets planted in a copper pot," said Tink and Lily.

"Thank you, fairies! You have given me so much inspiration!" Bess exclaimed. "Wait! That's it!"

Bess got to work right away.

Grabbing her biggest brush, Bess flew over to the long wall of her art studio and began to paint.

Just as the sun was about to set, Bess flew back to take a good look at the wall. She had painted her five fairy friends—her biggest and brightest inspirations!

"What a beautiful mural," said Lily.

"I love the colors," Beck added.

"The copper pot looks especially nice." Tink winked.

51

Bess grinned. "Thank you all for being my true inspirations! I could not ask for better fairy friends than you!" she said.

The fairies gathered for a big hug. They were so flattered by Bess's painting and happy for the reminder of what great friends they were.

The End

A Snowy Surprise

It was a warm, sunny day in Pixie Hollow. Tinker Bell, Rani, and two garden-talent fairies were canoeing at the lake when Vidia suddenly swooped down.

"Good morning, petal-heads," Vidia teased. "Canoeing looks so boring!"

With that, she circled over the canoe, causing it to sway back and forth.

"Vidia!" Tink cried. "One day you will learn to appreciate other fairy talents."

Vidia laughed. "That will happen when it snows in Pixie Hollow. And I don't mean the Winter Woods."

Lily was the first fairy to notice something odd in Pixie Hollow. She was taking care of flowers in her garden and began to shiver.

"That's weird," Lily said. "Looks like rain, but it's so cold!"

Rosetta flew to Lily's garden. "Look, Lily!" she exclaimed. She held out a lacy white crystal for Lily to see, but it melted into a puddle right before their eyes. "What in Never Land is going on?" asked Lily.

Before long, a thin layer of white covered the ground. The fairies were puzzled by the lacy white flakes but also curious. Fairies tried to catch the flakes, roll them into balls, and even taste them!

"Rather bland," said Dulcie. "I thought they would be sweet like sugar!"

"Well, you can make shapes with them," added Prilla.

Tinker Bell flew over. She knew exactly what the lacy white flakes were.

"It's snow!" Tink cried.

"Snow?" asked all the fairies.

"What do we do in the snow?" asked Lily.

"We play in it, of course!" said Tinker Bell.

Just then, Prilla scooped up a handful of snow and tossed it toward Tink.

Tink laughed. "Watch out, Prilla! I'll get you back!"

Soon, all the fairies had joined in for a snowball toss.

Before long, the fairies realized the snow was too cold to play in forever. They needed a way to keep warm.

The sewing-talent fairies got to work making hats and scarves, and the cobbler-talent fairies made boots out of moss and leaves.

65

While waiting for the hats and scarves to be finished, Fira flew to the Pixie Dust Tree. She thought there might be something there to keep the fairies warm.

"Moon and stars!" Fira exclaimed. "The great tree is sparkling like a palace of jewels! The fairies are going to love it!"

The art-talent fairies had already discovered their love for the snow.

"You can sculpt with it!" shouted Bess as she built a snow-fairy, complete with wings made from frosted spiderwebs. "This one is you, Tinker Bell!"

"I love it!" Tink exclaimed.

Over at the stream, the fairies found that the usually
running water was now smooth like glass.

"Look," said Rani. "It's hard...and slippery, too!" She
stepped out onto the surface and began to glide. "I'm skating!"
she cried.

The cold snow had made a skating rink in Pixie Hollow!

By midafternoon, every fairy in Pixie Hollow was enjoying the snow!

"This is so exciting!" Tink shouted while sledding in a silver spoon. "But where is all this snow coming from?"

"We may never know." Terence shrugged. "Let's just enjoy it while it's here!"

In the meadow, the fast-flying fairies were whipping down the snow-covered slopes. They had made their sleds out of large green leaves.

"Care for a race?" Vidia asked. She could never resist a little competition.

"Sure," the other fairies shouted.

"Go!" Vidia shouted. "Can't catch me! I'm the fastest fairy in Pixie Hollow."

"I win," Vidia shouted when she reached the bottom of the slope.

"Great job," said Rani. "It looks like you are having fun."

"I am," Vidia answered. "Why do you care?"

Rani pointed to the sky. The water-talent fairies were turning raindrops into snow. "You said you would appreciate other talents when it snowed in Pixie Hollow," she said. "You can thank the water fairies for all the fun you're having."

"I guess," Vidia said. "But it's not *that* much fun."

"You know, Rani," Tink said, hiding behind a plant, "I think Vidia appreciates your talent as well as the other fairies' talents."

Rani smiled. "I agree, even though Vidia will never admit it."

The End

The Messy Mystery

One morning, Tinker Bell arrived at her workshop to find that it was a complete mess!

"Oh my!" Tink gasped. "Someone was here while I was gone, and they took the silver measuring spoons I was fixing."

She thought about who might do such a thing. Maybe the baking fairies needed the spoons in a hurry.

"Those spoons aren't fixed yet," she said out loud. "I'd better go to the kitchen and warn the fairies!"

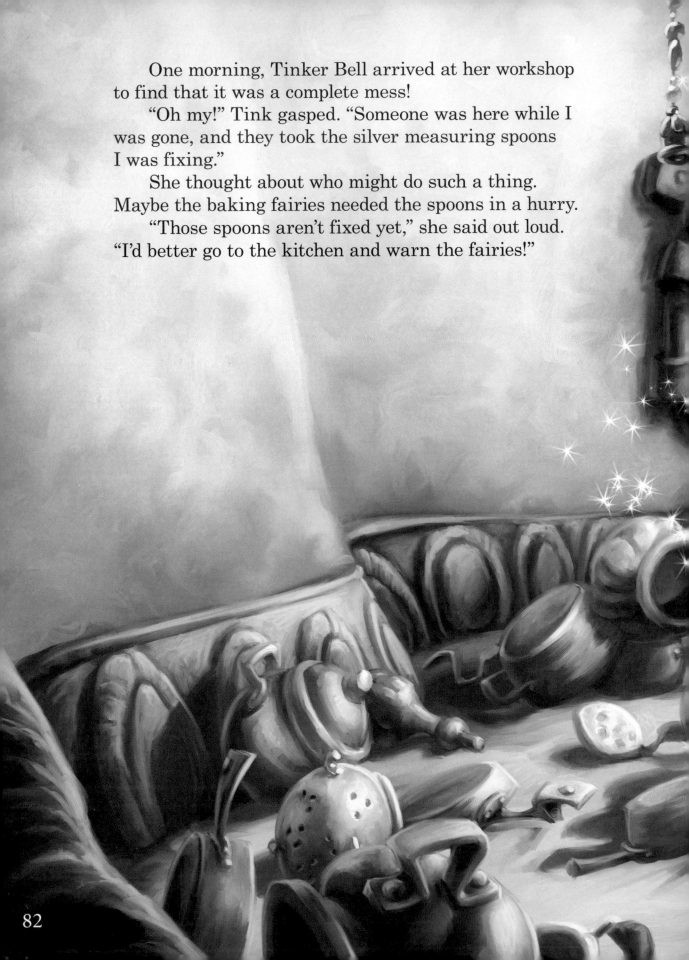

When Tink arrived in the kitchen, she found
Dulcie and the other baking fairies in a mess themselves.

"Someone has made a mess of the kitchen," Dulcie
complained. "And that's not all. Three gingerbread cupcakes
were stolen."

"Or eaten," Tink said. "Look at all those crumbs on the
floor. Let's look in the tearoom. Whoever ate those cupcakes
might need to wash them down with a cup of tea."

Tink and Dulcie arrived in the tearoom. There, they found Fira and Prilla in yet another huge mess.

"What happened here?" Tink asked.

"We don't know," Fira answered. "When we came in, the tables were a mess, the chairs were knocked down, and tea was spilled everywhere!"

"Who is making all this mischief? And why?" asked Dulcie.

"I don't know," Tink answered. "But I am going to find out! Dulcie, you and Fira stay here and keep watch. Prilla, you and I will follow every clue we have and get to the bottom of this!"

The fairies agreed.

"To start, let's follow that sugar!" cried Tink.

Tink and Prilla followed the trail of sugar out of the tearoom, then up the staircase, around the long hallway, and then…right up to Beck's bedroom door!

Beck, an animal-talent fairy, usually kept her door shut and her room tidy.

"Something isn't right," Tink said. "Let's peek inside and make sure everything is okay."

Beck wasn't in her room, but there was sugar everywhere. Tink spotted her silver mixing spoons!

"Do you think Beck made the mess in your workshop, the kitchen, and the tearoom?" Prilla asked.

"I am positive it wasn't her," Tink replied. "There is something mysterious going on. Come on! Let's gather more clues!"

Tink and Prilla flew to Bess's art studio to search for clues.

Bess was distracted by a butterfly behind some bushes, but they spotted Beck! She looked over both her shoulders and darted in and out of the bushes. It looked like she was hiding!

"Why is Beck sneaking around like that?" Prilla wondered.

"It's very odd," Tink said. "We should catch up with her and find out!"

Before Tink and Prilla got close, Beck zipped away faster than a fast-flying fairy!

"Whoa!" Prilla gasped. "Look! Bess is back in her studio." The two fairies flew over.

"Oh no!" Bess cried. "My studio is a mess! The cake I was painting is gone, too!"

"The mess-making thief has struck again!" Prilla said.

"We have to go," Tink explained. "We will find your cake, I promise."

Tink and Prilla spotted Beck as they flew over Lily's garden. They hid behind a flower and decided what to do.

"How can we be sure Beck isn't the mess-making thief?" Prilla whispered. "We saw her outside Bess's studio right before the cake went missing."

"I don't think Beck had enough time to make that mess," Tink replied. "I just wish I knew what's going on."

In the blink of an eye, Beck sprang up.

"Aha! Caught you!" she shouted. But when she saw Tink and Prilla, she was surprised. "What are you doing here?"

"We were following you," Tink answered.

"Following me?" Beck asked. "Well, why?"

"Someone has been causing damage all over Pixie Hollow," replied Tink. "Things have also gone missing!"

"And the clues all point to you," Prilla said.

Beck grinned. "I need to show you both something."

Behind some tall grass, Beck showed Tink and Prilla the furry
friends causing all the trouble around Pixie Hollow.

"Come out, you silly little hedgehogs," Beck said. "I see you hiding!"

Tink and Prilla were surprised to see three baby hedgehogs rolling
around in the grass.

"We were playing hide-and-seek," Beck explained. "But these rascals kept getting away. I've been chasing them all morning, but it looks like they wore themselves out!"

"You should have asked for help," Tink said.

"Yeah," Beck replied. "But I thought I could do it myself."

"I have an idea that Prilla and I can help you with," Tink said. The three fairies built a little playpen for the baby hedgehogs.

"Now the hedgehogs can stay safe, and you can keep your eye on them, Beck!" Prilla explained.

"Fantastic!" Beck replied. "Well, it looks like you two solved the messy mystery!"

The End

Finders, Keepers

One day, Tinker Bell was flying across a stream when she saw a mysterious object beneath a large branch.

Tinker Bell was no stranger to collecting interesting and useful items, so she flew over to investigate! She balanced herself on the branch and wriggled the item loose!

"What is it?" she wondered aloud. "Well, its shape is very strange, and it's too large to be useful to me."

Tink flew off, leaving the unknown object behind.

At that moment, Beck was hurrying along the stream. She was on her way to visit the squirrel family. She was running so fast when...

Thump!

She tripped and fell to the ground. "Ow," she cried. "What in the world is this? And why is it lying here?"

Suddenly, Beck had an idea. She could bring this object to the squirrel family as a gift!

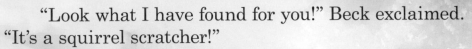

"Look what I have found for you!" Beck exclaimed. "It's a squirrel scratcher!"

The squirrel family gathered. They each waited their turn as Beck gave little scratches behind their ears, on their tails, and on their round bellies.

When all the squirrels were scratched, Beck had to go home. "I'll bring the scratcher again next time," she promised.

"Now, where can I put this and keep it safe?" Beck said. The scratcher was too big to keep in her room.

At last, she decided to keep it in the roots of the Pixie Dust Tree. "This should work." Beck smiled.

Meanwhile, back at her workshop, Tinker Bell was having some trouble. She was trying to wash a tall, narrow pot that she had just finished fixing.

"What's wrong?" asked Terence. "I could hear you scowling from the other room."

"It's this pot," Tink said. "It's so tall that I can't clean the bottom. My arm doesn't reach."

"You need something like this," Terence said, drawing in the air with pixie dust. He sketched an outline of a brush with a long handle.

Tinker Bell blinked in astonishment. Terence's pixie dust drawing looked exactly like…the object stuck in the stream!

"Come on!" Tink yelped. "We need to get to the stream!"

Not too far away, Lily was resting on a high branch of the Pixie Dust Tree. She had spent the entire morning scaring shimmer beetles away from her garden. The beetles loved to eat her beautiful purple flowers.

Just as she was about to sip some dew from a leaf, she spotted something below.

"What is that?" Lily asked. "It's as tall as a fairy! Hmm…I have an idea."

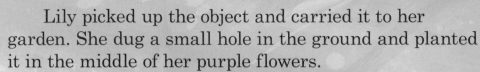

Lily picked up the object and carried it to her garden. She dug a small hole in the ground and planted it in the middle of her purple flowers.

Next, she added dry grass blades for hair, plucked a blossom to use as a dress, and added her sun hat for the finishing touch.

"That is an outstanding scare-bug, if I do say so myself," she said proudly. "It will definitely keep the shimmer beetles away!"

Back at the stream, Tink and Terence were looking everywhere for the tall odd-shaped object.

"I wish I had known it would be so useful when I first saw it," Tink said sadly. "Hey! Did you hear that, Terence?"

"Tink! Terence!" Beck shouted. She flew toward them.

"What's wrong?" Tink and Terence asked.

"I left a squirrel scratcher outside the Pixie Dust Tree, and now it's missing!" Beck exclaimed. "Have you seen it?"

"No," Tink replied. "But I am also looking for something. Let's all search together!"

Beck, Tink, and Terence flew over Lily's garden and spotted something peculiar.

Terence flew closer to get a better look.

"What is this thing?" he asked.

"You found my squirrel scratcher!" Beck exclaimed.

"That isn't your squirrel scratcher," Tink said, flying closer. "I found it this morning. It's my long-handled pot scrubber!"

"No," Lily added. "It's my new scare-bug!"

Swiftly, a dark shadow flew over the garden, and the fairies stopped arguing.

It was a hawk—and it was coming right for them!

"Look out!" Terence shouted.

The fairies scattered as the hawk swooped down. It reached out its sharp claws...and grabbed the scare-bug! Then, with a screech, it flew away.

"Is everyone all right?" Tink asked. She looked around carefully and came out from the daffodil she was hiding in.

"What just happened?" Terence asked.

"I think that hawk just took our back-scratching, pot-scrubbing, beetle-scaring thing!" Beck exclaimed.

The fairies laughed.

"I wonder what that thing is really for," Lily said.

"I guess we'll never know," Tink replied.

The End

The Pixie Mix-Up

One morning, just after dawn, Tinker Bell was hard at work fixing the weather compass at the top of the Pixie Dust Tree.

She was tapping the last nail into place when a warm breeze swept through the tree.

"Ah." Tink sighed. "There is nothing like a spring breeze in Pixie Hollow."

The spring breeze drifted through the windows of the Pixie Dust Tree, waking up all the fairies.

Soon the fairies were flittering about—cleaning the windows, hanging the flower petal curtains, and making Pixie Hollow sparkle. It was time for spring-cleaning!

Tink was on her way to tidy up her workshop when she heard someone call her name.

"Tink! Down here!" Lily shouted. "I'm planting new flowers, but I need to get my garden rake. Would you mind watering the flowers while I'm gone?"

Tink was eager to get to her workshop, but watering the flowers would only take a minute.

"Sure," she answered. "I'd love to help out."

Tink watered the first flower and the next and the
next. *Drip, drip, drip.*

"This watering can is so slow!" She sighed with
frustration. "It will take all day to water these flowers."

But being a tinker fairy, she had an idea!

Within moments, Tinker Bell had built a supersized sprinkler! She hung a group of watering cans to a strong vine and—voilà! When she pulled the vine, the watering cans tipped and gently showered the flowers.

Tink smiled. This job would be done in no time. Then she would be off to her workshop.

Lily was hurrying across the courtyard on her way to her garden shed when Rani stopped her.

"Oh, Lily!" Rani exclaimed. "Could you please do me a favor?"

"Of course," Lily answered.

"Great!" Rani said. "I am washing the courtyard, but I have run out of soap. Could you keep an eye on things while I go get more?"

Lily nodded. It sounded easy enough.

One minute passed, then two, then three. Lily was eager to get back to her flowers! She wished there was a quicker way she could help Rani.

In her garden, Lily helped the flowers grow by whispering words of encouragement. Why couldn't she do the same with the soap bubbles?

"Come on, little bubbles. Get bigger! You can do it!" she whispered.

The bubbles began to grow right away. Lily smiled.

Inside the Pixie Dust Tree, Rani hurried down the hall. As she passed through the tearoom, she heard a strange sound.

"Chee-chee!"

Rani found Beck dusting the tearoom with the help of her squirrel friends.

"Rani!" Beck cried. "I am so glad to see you. I need to gather some nuts for the squirrels. Would you be able to help point out the dusty spots while I go find their treats?"

"Of course, Beck," Rani said. "I am happy to help."

Rani watched the squirrels and helped them with their chores. She pointed out the spots that needed dusting, but the squirrels weren't listening.

"At this rate, the dusting is never going to get done!" Rani cried. She wished she could speak squirrel. "Maybe I can imitate Beck: Chi-chi!"

The squirrels froze.

"They understand me!" Rani shouted. She kept talking squirrel, hoping to get the work done quickly.

149

But the squirrels started running around the tearoom, knocking over all the tables and chairs.

Beck flew back from gathering nuts. "What's going on?" she cried.

"I was just trying to tell them to dust over there," Rani said. "Like this: Chi-chi!"

"That doesn't mean 'Dust over there!'" Beck shouted. "That means 'Look out for that hawk!'"

The squirrels raced out of the tearoom in a panicked frenzy!

When the fairies reached the door, they looked out to see a huge mess! The squirrels slipped on the bubbles, skidded across the courtyard, and flew in the air, crashing right into Tink's watering-can sprinkler.

"Oh no!" Tink cried.

"This is not good," Rani added.

When the mayhem finally settled down, the fairies looked around the courtyard. Standing before them was a group of angry fairies.

"The laundry is soggy, the flowers are soapy, and the courtyard is a mess!" the angriest fairy shouted.

"I didn't mean to scare the squirrels," Rani said.

"I guess I made the bubbles too big," Lily admitted.

"Look," Tink interrupted. "This was all an honest mistake. Now, let's work together and clean up Pixie Hollow!"

And that is exactly what the fairies did.
In no time, Pixie Hollow shimmered and shined.

The End

The Great Fairy Campout

Tinker Bell was sitting in a flower patch enjoying the summer sunshine when a delicious scent tickled her nose.

Somewhere, a baking fairy was roasting marshmallows to add to a mouthwatering treat!

The smell reminded Tink of the campouts she used to go on with Peter Pan.

"Oh! A campout!" she exclaimed. "That's a wonderful idea!"

Quickly, Tink flew to the Pixie Dust Tree kitchen.

"I am going on a campout," Tink told Dulcie. "And I need to pack some food."

"What's a campout?" Dulcie asked.

"Well, it's when you take home away from home," Tink explained. "You pitch a tent, build a fire, and cook your dinner…all outside under the stars!"

"Sounds fun!" Dulcie cried. "Can I come, too?"

"The more the merrier," Tink replied. And the two fairies started packing some food.

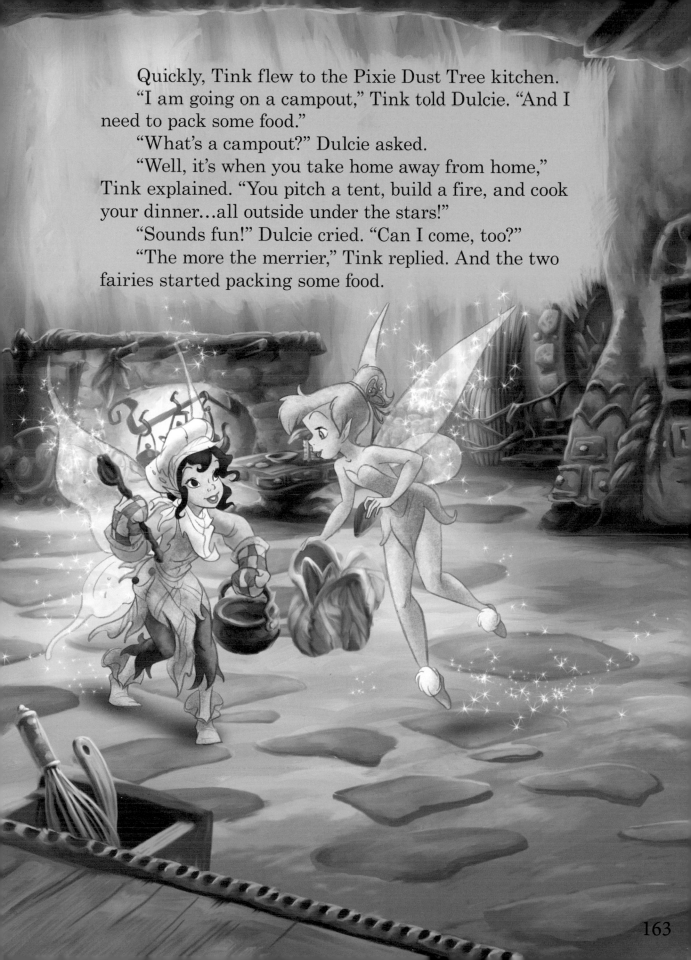

Tink's plan for a campout spread throughout Pixie Hollow!
Soon, all the fairies were aflutter with activity!

"Is everyone ready?" Tink asked.

"Ready!" shouted all the fairies.

"Er...ready!" Dulcie said. She was carrying the biggest leaf-pack Tink had ever seen!

"That is an awfully big pack," Tink said. "What is in there?"

"It's all my baking tools!" Dulcie replied.

"You're going to carry them the whole way?" Tink asked.

"It wouldn't be a home-away-from-home trip without them," said Dulcie.

"All right," Tink said. "But I think it's going to get very heavy very fast! I hope you can keep up."

The fairies set off to find the best campsite, but it wasn't easy. The water-talent fairies hoped to camp near a stream, while the forest-talent fairies wanted to pitch their tents in the deep woods.

"Can't we just stop here?" Dulcie panted.

"No." Tinker Bell shook her head. "We have to keep looking!"

After a few more minutes of searching, the
fairies found a perfectly sunlit area of the woods
to set up their camp in.

Tink stopped and looked around. "It's close to the deep woods. It's close to the stream, and best of all, we can gaze up at the stars! It's perfect!"

All the other fairies agreed.

169

"Now what?" Lily asked as they put down their packs.

"Well, first," Tink replied, "we set up the camp! We should pitch our tents, organize the games, and find a place to eat."

The fairies set up their tents in a perfect circle. Once they finished, they played games until the sun set.

The camp was cozy and aglow with the light of the fire and the lanterns.

Soon the fairies were hungry.

The fairies ate roasted chestnuts, wild strawberries, and other foods they found in the forest.

"Mmmm." Rani sighed. "This is a delicious dinner."

"Chestnuts are always great cooked over a campfire," Tink said. "But it feels like something is missing. I just don't know what."

As soon as dinner was finished, the storytelling-talent fairies gathered around the campfire.

"Once upon a time," a storyteller began, "there was a ladybug who loved to dance...."

"No, no, no," Tink interrupted. "Campfire stories are supposed to be spooky."

"Spooky?" asked the fairies.

"Yes, like about ghosts! Boo!" Tink shouted behind the storytelling fairy, startling him.

"I know a spooky story," said Beck, leaping to her feet. "It's about a snake…with two heads!" Beck made shadow puppets on a stone to illustrate.

"Eek!" the fairies exclaimed.

"I know one, too!" Bess cried. "It's about a ghost, and the ghost is an owl!"

"Ooh!" gasped the fairies.

Tinker Bell was next. "Have you heard the legend of the evil pirate captain?" she asked.

The fairies yelped and moved closer together.

"He had an iron hook for a hand!" Tink exclaimed.

"Oh my," Lily said.

Clank! Crash!

The fairies hurried to their petal tents.

"It's the owl ghost!" one fairy shouted.

But Tinker Bell wasn't afraid, and she wasn't going to let anything get in the way of her camping. She lit a small stick and crept over to the edge of the campsite.

It was Dulcie!

"Dulcie, where have you been?" Tink asked.

"I got lost," she replied, "and it took me forever to find the campsite. It's dark out there, and my bag is so heavy!" She looked around. "Where is everybody?"

"Hiding," Tink admitted. "They thought you were an owl ghost, so they hid in their tents."

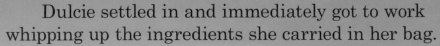

Dulcie settled in and immediately got to work whipping up the ingredients she carried in her bag.

"I made a special campfire cake," Dulcie announced. "I told Tink I couldn't make a home away from home without baking."

Tink replied with a smile, "This has been the best camping trip ever!"

The End

The Perfect Pumpkin Hunt

It was fall in Pixie Hollow. Prilla loved the fall because there were always so many fun things to do! She watched squirrels hunt for nuts and chased falling leaves.

"Wee!" Prilla cried as she jumped onto a big oak leaf. She rode the leaf as it drifted to the ground.

Just as Prilla's leaf touched the ground, Queen Clarion flew over.

"Prilla, tonight is the Fall Celebration, and I need your help," Queen Clarion said. "Do you think you can find the most wonderful pumpkin for the celebration?"

"Of course!" Prilla exclaimed. "I love the Fall Celebration!"

Queen Clarion and Prilla flew back to the Pixie Dust Tree together.

All around them, fairies were getting ready for the celebration. Party-talent fairies hung streamers made of grapevines while music-talent fairies tuned reed whistles and walnut drums.

"It's so magical," Prilla said. "I can't wait for the music, the dancing, and the delicious treats."

The two fairies made their way to the kitchen. Dulcie and the baking-talent fairies were baking apple pies and pear pies.

Every fairy in Pixie Hollow had a job to do in order to make this the best Fall Celebration.

"There isn't much time," Queen Clarion announced. "You should start your pumpkin hunt soon."

"I will hurry," Prilla replied. "You have nothing to worry about."

With that, she flew off. Prilla was determined to find the perfect pumpkin.

Just past the Pixie Dust Tree, Lily was cleaning her garden. She was trying to lift a big orange leaf, but she couldn't do it alone.

"Can you help me?" Lily asked.

"Sure," Prilla answered. "But then I must be on my way. I have to find the perfect pumpkin for the Fall Celebration."

Together, Prilla and Lily lifted the leaf and moved it out of the garden.

"Wow, that was a huge help," Lily said. "I really would not have been able to lift that without you!"

"You're welcome," Prilla responded. "Now I have to go!"
She waved good-bye to her friend.

As Prilla flew toward the pumpkin patch, she noticed Beck placing nuts into baskets with a squirrel friend.

"Hello, Beck," Prilla said. "What are you doing with all those nuts?"

"We are sorting them!" Beck explained. "Hazelnuts go in the yellow basket and walnuts go in the green basket."

There were so many nuts to sort! Prilla decided to help Beck and the squirrel.

Quickly, they organized the nuts into the appropriate baskets.

"Thank you!" cried Beck. "This would have taken us forever without your help."

"You're welcome," Prilla said. "It was fun!"

Prilla took off. She still had to find her perfect pumpkin—and fast!

From above, Prilla saw Tinker Bell and Pluck working in the meadow. They were building a wagon. Tink fixed an acorn-cap wheel while Pluck loaded the wagon with hay.

Prilla flew down to take a closer look. "This will be great for hayrides," she said. "But it looks like a lot of hard work for just two fairies."

"Would you mind helping us out?" Tinker Bell asked.

"Sure!" Prilla replied.

Prilla held the acorn-cap wheel in place for Tink and helped Pluck carry hay to the wagon. Finally, the wagon was finished!

The sun was starting to set, so Prilla took off once again toward the pumpkin patch.

"It was so much fun helping with the wagon," Prilla said. "But I must go! See you again soon."

Prilla flew as fast as she could!

When she finally arrived at the pumpkin patch, she gasped. There were pumpkins as far as she could see! How was she ever going to find the most perfect pumpkin?

Prilla flew around the patch from pumpkin to pumpkin.

One pumpkin was too green.

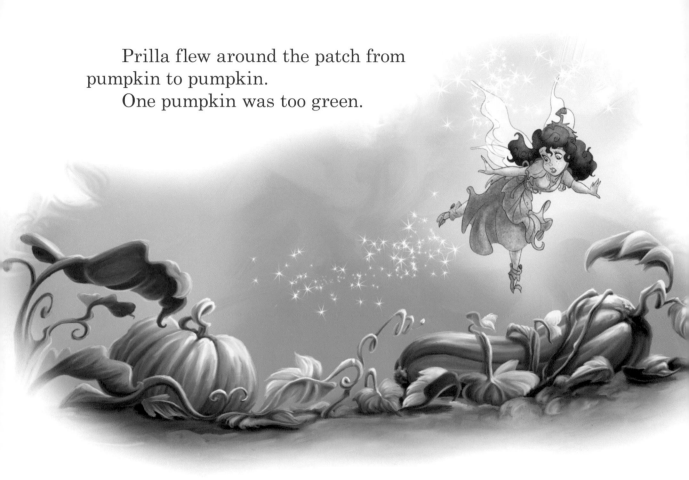

One was too small.

Another was too bumpy.

And one was too smelly!
Not one of the pumpkins was right, and Prilla was
running out of time!

Suddenly, Prilla spotted a pumpkin at the edge of the patch. It was big, round, and bright orange.

It was perfect!

"It's as smooth as glass," Prilla said. "It's flawless!"

Prilla couldn't wait to show it to everyone at the celebration.

"They're going to love it!" she shouted.

There was just one problem.
This pumpkin was *heavy*!
Prilla pushed.

She pulled.

214

She tugged with a vine.

The pumpkin
would not budge!

Prilla sat down to rest. She was worried she wasn't
going to be able to make it to the Fall Celebration.

"It's almost sunset!" she cried. "No one will see my
perfect pumpkin."

Then, Prilla heard something.

"We'll help you!" some voices called.
It was Tink, Lily, Pluck, Beck, and Beck's
squirrel friend, too!

"You helped us," Tinker Bell said. "Now it is our turn to help you!"

Together, the fairies rolled the pumpkin onto Tink and Pluck's wagon. Then, Beck's squirrel friend pulled the wagon back to Pixie Hollow.

"The pumpkin is moving," Prilla yelled.
"Thank you, friends!"

As the sun set, the wagon rolled into the courtyard.
The fairies gasped. The courtyard looked beautiful!
The fireflies twinkled, colorful leaves covered the ground,
and dried corncobs hung from cotton-ball carriers.
Prilla's perfect pumpkin was going to be a wonderful
finishing touch!

Prilla stopped the wagon, and the fairies of Pixie Hollow flew over to help roll the pumpkin onto the ground.

Queen Clarion flew over, too. "That really is the biggest, brightest, most beautiful pumpkin I have ever seen," she said. "Let the Fall Celebration begin!"

Prilla hugged her fairy friends.
"I found the perfect pumpkin!" she cried.
"But it could not have happened without my perfect friends!"

The End

Beck's Bunny Secret

Beck looked over her left shoulder, then over her right shoulder. Next she looked behind her. She needed to make sure she was alone.

She parted the blades of grass and slipped inside a hidden corner of the meadow.

Beck had a very fuzzy secret. It was a baby bunny named Bitty!

She was taking care of the baby bunny because he was separated from his bunny family.

"I must keep you hidden in the meadow," Beck said to Bitty. "It is safer for now." Beck stroked Bitty's soft ears and sang him a special lullaby.

Bitty wasn't the first stray animal Beck had taken care of.

First, there was the baby skunk. Rosetta was not happy about the skunk since he produced stinky scents everywhere he went!

"P-U!" Rosetta would cry.

Then there was the baby wart toad. He was very cute, but he made Beck's skin bumpy.

And of course, there was the egg Beck found in Brackle Swamp. She didn't know it would hatch a baby crocodile!

The little croc scared Terence and the other fairies! But she ended up being the sweetest baby crocodile.

During her next visit with Bitty, Beck was stroking the bunny's soft fur when she heard a voice calling her.

"Beck! Where are you?" called the voice.

Beck gasped. It was Fawn!

"Shhh," Beck told Bitty. "I don't want anyone to find you here."

Beck snuck out of the high grass and flew over to Fawn.
"There you are!" Fawn said.
Rustle, rustle, rustle.
"What's that noise?" Fawn asked.

Beck's face turned bright red. Bitty must have been hopping about!

Rustle, rustle, rustle.

Fawn pointed right at Bitty's hiding spot. "It's coming from that clump of grass!" she cried.

"I think that was just the wind," Beck told Fawn.

"Beck, I am no weather-talent fairy," Fawn said, "but even I can tell you there hasn't been a single gust of wind today!"

Fawn flew over to the tall grass.

"There is something going on over here," Fawn said.

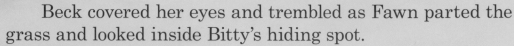

Beck covered her eyes and trembled as Fawn parted the grass and looked inside Bitty's hiding spot.

When Beck found the courage, she peeked through her fingers...but nothing was there. Bitty was gone!

"You were right, Beck," said Fawn.
"There isn't anything behind this grass."
With that, Fawn flew away.

As soon as Fawn was gone, Beck started searching for Bitty. Where would a baby bunny go?

"Bunnies love to eat," Beck thought aloud. "Maybe he is in the lettuce patch!"

No Bitty.

"Hmm, maybe he is in the carrot patch!" Beck cried.
There was still no sign of Bitty.

Beck looked at the peas...

and the beans...

and then the beets.

No baby bunny teeth marks could be found!

Beck flew to the Fairy Dust Mill and found
Terence filling pumpkin shells with pixie dust.

"Has anyone been eating your pumpkin shells?"
Beck asked.

Terence shook his head. "Is everything okay?"
he asked.

"Yes, but I have to run!" Beck said as she took
off in a hurry.

"Hmm," Beck thought. "Maybe Bitty wasn't hungry…perhaps he was thirsty!"

Beck flew to the stream and found Rani making a leaf boat.

"Have you seen any paw prints nearby?" Beck asked.

"No," Rani replied. "But if I do, I will let you know right away."

"Thanks," Beck said.

Beck was getting nervous. Where could Bitty be?

She stopped by Brother Dove's nest, but there was no bunny there.

She checked Tinker Bell's workshop. No Bitty there, either.

She dropped by Bess's
art studio.

And she searched
Lily's garden.
She couldn't find
Bitty anywhere!

Beck realized she had one more place to look! She flew to the tearoom right away!

Dulcie was in a state of panic! "Something has been nibbling my carrot cake!" she cried. "Look at the huge chunk missing from one side!"

It had to be Bitty, Beck thought.

"Oh my," Beck said. "Let me look around the tearoom for you."

Beck searched the tearoom high and low for Bitty, but she didn't find the baby bunny anywhere!

She did find Prilla with icing all over her face and a piece of cake in her hands.

"It's just so good," Prilla said. "I had to sneak a piece before anyone else."

Beck sighed. She really thought she had found Bitty.

Beck had looked everywhere, but there was no sign of Bitty! She was sad. What was she going to do?

"This is just terrible," she cried. "Bitty is all alone somewhere in Pixie Hollow. How did this ever happen?"

As Beck flew over the meadow, she heard a familiar sound coming from the small clover patch.

Rustle, rustle, rustle.

"Could it be?" she cried out.

In a blink, she flew over to the clover patch and looked inside.

Inside were Fawn and Bitty! Fawn was using a clover to play with Bitty and petting the baby bunny's very soft fur. Beck was so relieved. Bitty was safe with her friend.

"Fawn!" Beck called out.

"Oh, Beck," Fawn responded. "I have been taking care of Bitty for you. He told me how you have been making sure he is safe. I kept him protected in this clover patch."

"Thank you!" Beck said. "I was searching all over Pixie Hollow. I thought I lost Bitty! I am so happy to see him again."

Out of nowhere, Beck started laughing uncontrollably.
"What is so funny?" Fawn wondered.

"Oh," Beck started. "I was imagining us both running all over Pixie Hollow just missing each other! We must have passed each other all day!"

Fawn laughed. "That is pretty silly!"

Beck and Fawn linked their hands over Bitty and came together for a big, fuzzy hug.

"I have an idea," Fawn said. "Let's take care of Bitty together. And next time, you should let the fairies know about your foster animals. That way, we can help you take care of them!"

"Great idea!" Beck smiled.

The End

Read these other
Disney Fairies storybooks!